Tough AS

Lace

Lexi Bruce

An imprint of Enslow Publishing

WEST 44 BOOKS™

Please visit our website, www.west44books.com.
For a free color catalog of all our high-quality books,
call toll free 1-800-398-2504.

Cataloging-in-Publication Data

Names: Bruce, Lexi.
Title: Tough as lace / Lexi Bruce.
Description: New York : West 44, 2022.
Identifiers: ISBN 9781978595514 (pbk.) | ISBN 9781978595651
(library bound) | ISBN 9781978595538 (ebook)
Subjects: LCSH: Poetry, American--21st century. | English poetry. |
Young adult poetry, American. | Poetry, Modern--21st century.
Classification: LCC PS586.3 T684 2022 | DDC 811'.60809282--dc23

First Edition

Published in 2022 by
Enslow Publishing LLC
29 East 21st Street
New York, NY 10010

Editor: Caitie McAneney
Interior Layout: Rachel Rising

Photo Credits: Cover, pp. 1, 2-184 Sylvvie/Shutterstock.com; pp.43,
49, 51, 68, 69, 71, 79, 93, 93, 95, 97, 105, 108, 109, 111, 113, 115, 116,
123, 125, 127, 131, 135, 139, 151-153, 156, 166, 167, 169 Kraska/
Shutterstock.com.

Printed in the United States of America

CPSIA compliance information: Batch #CS22W44: For further information contact
Enslow Publishing LLC, New York, New York at 1-800-398-2504.

To Dan, who reminded me how to not panic over literally everything, all the time, and whose presence (and sarcasm) always brings me peace.

P.S. Breakfast next Wednesday?

Who I Am

My name is Lacey,
but I am not
like lace.

I am bruises.
I am turf burn.
I am mud-caked cleats
and I am sweat stains.

I am lightning
on the lacrosse field.
Swerving
around defenders
and shooting
the ball past goalies.

I am not
delicate and for show.
I am not so special
that mud will ruin me.

I am not here
to look pretty
at the dining room table.

I am here to do
what I have to.

I am here to win.

Winning Together

After Friday afternoon practice,
I walk with my best friend–
and goalie–Jenna.
Head over to our favorite
hangout spot,
Rosie's Juice and Smoothie Bar.
Meet up with
my boyfriend,
Owen.

I notice him as soon
as we walk in.
He looks up
and waves at us.
Then runs
his fingers
through his messy,
dark hair.

He's sitting at a table,
sipping a mango-berry smoothie.
Reading *The Glass Menagerie*
for English on Monday.

He already ordered
my favorite smoothie for me,
mixed berry
with lots of ginger.

He closes his book
and kisses me
when I sit down
next to him.

Jenna goes up to the counter
to place her order.

"How was practice?"
Owen asks
as I take my first
sip of the smoothie.

"Really great,"
I say.
"I think
this is gonna be
my season!"

"I can't believe
I'm dating the greatest
lacrosse star
in the state,"
Owen says.

"Oh, cut it out.
You know that's
not true. I'm really only
the *second* greatest
lacrosse star
in New York,"
I joke and kiss him.

We always tease
over which one of us
is a better player.

"Nope, you're definitely
the very best, Lace.
You're number one,
I swear.
Lacrosse my heart
and hope to die."

He winks.

I'd never tell him,
but his bad puns
are one of
my favorite
things
in the world.

I roll my eyes
and smile at him.
I love that he means it
when he tells me
I'm the best.

"So, how was the student
government meeting today?"
I ask.
Owen is the president
of our school's chapter
of Amnesty International.

"It was good,"
he says.
"We voted
on a few things.
I found out that
our club is going
to host a speaker
for the whole school."

"Oh my gosh,
that's so great!"
I say,
and hug him.

Owen has been trying
to get a speaker to come
to our school
since last year.

This is a big win for him.

We are both winning
lately.

A Perfect Trio

Jenna comes back with
her order—a peanut butter
and banana smoothie bowl
topped with granola.

She pulls her sketchbook
and pencils out of her bag.
Starts drawing
while we talk about
spring break
next month.

Jenna barely looks up
from her work.
Draws even as
she starts talking
about going
to visit family
in Florida.

As long as
I've known her—
which feels like
my whole life—
she's always
kept a sketchbook
nearby.
She's always sketching
and doodling
whenever possible.

Even the notes
she takes at school
are surrounded
by drawings
all around
the margins.

Right now,
she's getting ready
to put some of her work
up on the walls
at the coffee shop
where I work.

It will be her first
real art show.
I'm really excited
to see her art
when I walk into work.

Hanging with Owen and Jenna
is so easy

My life seems perfect
when I'm with them.

Not a Perfect Daughter

The next morning,
Mom drives me
to my SAT
prep class.

I totally bombed
the SAT
the first time
I took it in the fall.

"Lace, you really have to
focus on this,"
Mom says,
as I buckle my seat belt.
It's too early for lectures.
"I know you think
that lacrosse is
your thing, but
you need to really start
thinking about your future."

"I know," I say.

And I do know.
I know I'll need more
than lacrosse
to have a future.
Does she think I liked
scoring so low on
the SAT?

Does she think
I like feeling like
I've failed her
as her daughter?

Like I have no future
at all?

"I know
you're not dumb,"
Mom says.
"But I worry that
this lacrosse thing
is taking your
focus away
from more important
things."

I might be MVP
on the team that
beats all other teams—
but to my mom,

I'm a failure.

Luck

Today's the last
prep class before
I take the SAT again
next month.

"Remember," she says,
as I get out of the car.
"Aim for a perfect score!"

No pressure.

"And, Lace? Good luck!"

She's never wished me
good luck
before a lacrosse game.

And that's all
I've ever
really
wanted.

SAT Practice

I'm sitting
at a desk, with my
number two pencil.
Waiting for the instructor
to hand out
practice tests.

He lays down
the paper
in front of me.

"You may begin,"
he says,
as we all flip
our pages.

I hear
pencil on paper
as everyone begins.

I read
the first math question
three times.

I write
the equation
on the paper.
I circle
bubble A
on the sheet.

I check
my work
to be positive.

But this time,
it comes out
to be bubble C
on the answer sheet.

Oh no.
Which is it?

Not a good start
to the test.

And then
it happens.

I Fall Apart

My heart
starts to beat
like I've just run
back and forth
across the field.

I'm breathing hard,
but I'm sitting still.

I grip
the edge of the desk
until my fingers
ache.

My stomach
starts to feel
all wobbly,
and my head
starts to spin.

It feels like when
I've been
playing too hard
without any water.

I reach down
for my water bottle
and take a sip,
but that only makes
my stomach
feel worse.

I look
at the clock
on the wall
and see that
almost no time
has passed.

I hear
the pencils on paper
and the paper rustling,
and it makes
my head spin worse.

I pick up my pencil
and look down
at my paper.

The numbers swim
before my eyes.

What is happening to me?!

If I can't even pass
this stupid
practice test,
how am I going
to pass the real thing?

My heart keeps racing.

I can't even focus
on what
the next question
is asking.

It's like my brain
is stuck on

? ! ? ! ? !

I stand up
and feel dizzy,
like I might
fall over.
I put my hand
on the desk
to keep myself
upright.

"Ms. Stewart,"
the teacher says,
"please remain seated
until I call time."

"I'm sorry,"
I mumble,
rushing out
of the classroom.

I try to find
a safe space
to fall apart.

In the bathroom,
I rest my sweaty forehead
on the cold metal
of the stall door.

I lose track of time.
I don't know how long
I've been in here for.

Maybe
10 minutes,
maybe
an hour.

I Can't Stop Thinking

how badly
I'm going to fail
the SAT.

How I'll never
get into college.

How I'll never
make something
of myself.

How I'll be stuck
in Buffalo forever.

How I'll live my whole life
with my parents,
a big fat failure.

How everyone
must think I'm
crazy now.

Am I crazy?

Back to Normal(ish)

When my breath
finally slows down,
and my heartbeat too,
I go back
to the classroom.

When I get there,
the teacher is still
sitting at the desk
at the front of the room.

"Ms. Stewart,
are you OK?"
he asks.

"Yeah," I lie.
"My period just
hit me really hard
this month."

He doesn't ask
any more questions
after that.

Missed Texts

I pull my phone
out of my backpack
and see four missed texts
from my mom.

*I'm waiting
outside.*

*Did I get
the time wrong?
I'm here
to pick you up.*

??

*I just got a call
from a client,
and I have to go.
Text me if you
need anything!*

What Mom Does

Mom is an interior designer.

She makes things look
pretty
practical
perfect.

Our perfectly decorated house
is a testament to her designer *eye*.
And she recently signed
a local hotel as a client—
a big project.

But I'm kind of glad
that she's not here
to pick me up.

I don't want to hear
her judgments today.

All the ways I'm not
pretty
practical
perfect.

So I walk home alone,
shaky and weak.

Comfort

When I get home,
Dad is making
"super mac."
Boxed macaroni and cheese
with whatever vegetables
we have in the fridge.

It's what we
have for dinner
every Saturday,
ever since I was little.

It's also my favorite
comfort food.
And today
I could really
use some comfort.

Dad knows
how stressed
I've been
about the SATs.

"So, how did it go?"
he asks cheerfully.

"It was OK,"
I say.

I don't know how
to describe
how bad it was,
so I don't.

Dad doesn't press it.
And I'm relieved.

Just Try Harder

Mom is different.

When Mom
gets home,
she wants to know
how the class went.

How I feel about
the test and why
I was late leaving.

"Um, it didn't go
so great," I admit quietly.
"I don't think I can get
anything close to
a perfect score."

I hate admitting it.

"Of course
you can,"
Mom says.
"You just have to
try harder."

She hates that I'm not
as smart as her.
That I get Bs and Cs
instead of As.

How do you
tell someone
that you're
giving 110%
when you're still
falling short?

I don't want
to argue.

So I say,
"OK, Mom.
I'll try."

Lacrosse Practice

Outdoor
lacrosse practice
in March
in Buffalo
is always
a cold,
muddy mess.

But that just means
I can push
harder.
I can sweat
more.

I can
be the beast
I'm only
allowed to be
when I'm
on the turf.

Today
we're conditioning.

Coach has us running
back and forth
across the field.

Running laps
around the field.

Doing pushups
and burpees
in the mud.

For those
two hours
I focus on
pushing myself.

I focus on the
stretch
and the burn
in my muscles.

I don't have to think.
I feel good.

I just keep moving.
Nothing can
stop me.

No Mud Allowed

When I get home
from lacrosse practice,
I set down
my muddy
cleats outside the door.
Then I walk into
our spotless house.

It wouldn't
end well
for me if
I brought
them inside.

Mom is sitting
at the dining room table
typing away
on her laptop.

She looks up.

"You'd better not
be tracking mud
all over my clean floors,"
she says.
Looks at the mud
caked all over
my sweatpants.

I walk by her without
saying a word.

Pull the cuffs
of my pants up
so they don't
drag on the floor.

I go upstairs.
Change into pajama pants
and a clean sweatshirt.
Then head down
to the basement
to throw
my stinky,
muddy clothes
in the washer.

Homework Time

I go up
to my room
to do
my homework.

Chem first.

We're studying
acids and bases.

It all made sense
to me in class.

The pH scale.
How the formula works.

But now I turn on
my science calculator.

And I can't remember
which button to push.

One look
at the calculator
and my heart
starts beating
a little too fast
again.

Stupid, Stupid Me

I know
it's stupid
because
I knew
how to do this
earlier.

But now all I can
think about
is how stupid
I'll look in class
tomorrow
if I do this wrong.

And what if I'm just
that stupid?
And what if it means
that no college will
accept me?

And what if
I'm stuck here,
working in a coffee shop,
forever?

Stuck here
with my mom
telling me I'm never
good enough
clean enough
enough like her.

And now tears
are blurring
my vision.

I can't even see
the homework
question,
let alone remember
how to
do the thing.

And now
I'm sobbing
and breathing
fast.

I know I'm not
stupid.

But right now
I feel so
stupid.

I've been feeling
so stupid
all the time,
lately.
And I feel so stupid
for this awful
panic.

Not Supposed to Be

I kick butt
on the lacrosse field.
And I talk smack
at the girls
on the other team.

I pep my team up
with chants
and cheers.

I'm not supposed
to panic
or cry.

I'm supposed to
be the rock
that everyone else
can rely on.

And now
I'm not crying
about homework.

I'm crying
because I feel weak
for worrying.

And then I don't know
why I'm crying
anymore.

Who Am I?

I need to blow my nose.
I stand up
and go to the bathroom.

I catch sight of my face
in the bathroom mirror.

Red eyes.
Pink cheeks.
Snot running.

My hair's still a mess
from practice.

Staring myself in the eyes,
I burst into tears
all over again.

My mouth opens
in a silent sob.

It's like I'm choking
on my stress.

I grab a wad of toilet paper
and blow my nose.

And then I sit down
on the bathroom floor.

I hug my knees to my chest,
and cry.

I cry until
I have no more
tears left.

Just a Rough Day

I'm wiping the last
of my tears
from my eyes
when there's
a knock
on the bathroom
door.

"Lace?
Are you OK?"
Dad asks.

"I'm great,"
I say,
trying to sound
cheerful.

"Can I
come in?"
Dad asks.

"Um, sure,"
I say.

He opens the door,
finds me on the floor.
I stand up
and he wraps me
in a hug.

I start crying again.

"Oh, Lace,"
he says.
"What's wrong?"

"I can't focus
on my chem
homework.
I think something's
wrong with me,
Dad,"
I say between sobs.
It's hard for me
to admit.

"It's just a rough day, sport.
You'll be OK,"
Dad says.
"You always are.
Just keep trying
and you'll get it."

Slam

I wipe the tears
from my eyes,
grab a glass of water,
and take another
look at the homework.

As soon as I do,
my breath
comes faster
and my hands
are shaking.

I can't do this.

I don't know
how to do this.

I try to tell myself
that Dad is right,
and it's just
a rough day.

But it's not
just that.

I feel like
my whole future
rests on something
that I'm so bad at.

I can't remember
anything that Ms. Roberts
told us in class.

And I feel so freaking
stupid
right now.

I slam the textbook closed
and shove it into my backpack.

I don't want to even
think about chemistry.

Because I know
something isn't right
about this.

I want to understand
what's going on
with me.

Research

I open the web browser
on my phone. Type in:

trouble breathing
pain in chest
dizzy

The first page
tells me
I'm having a heart attack.
To call 911, now.

I scroll down
to another article.

Panic attack/anxiety.
This one makes more
sense.

I read the description:
racing heart
shortness of breath
sweating
shaking
light-headedness

YES.
If this is what
that was,
then there's
something
I can do about it.

Make It Better

After reading
a bunch of websites
about panic attacks,
I go downstairs
to tell my parents
what I found.

It's scary to tell them
about this,
but I do it anyway.

I tell them everything,
hardly taking a breath.

I want them to help me
make it better,
like when Mom used to
put Band-Aids on my
skinned knees.

"I really want
to figure this out,"
I say.

Eager for their response.

Their Response

Mom says,
"You're being
dramatic.
Don't *worry*
so much, Lace.
Really, just stop
stressing and focus
on the task at hand.
It's all in your head."

Dad nods.
"Your mom's right.
You're just psyching
yourself out."

Somehow that doesn't
make me feel any better.

Work

I work
at a coffee shop
called Bean City Coffee.
Just a weekend gig
to save up money
for college.

In case
the lacrosse scholarship
doesn't work out–

like Mom always says.

Mom doesn't like me
playing sports.

She says contact sports
aren't ladylike.

And Mom is *always*
a lady.

I take people's orders
at the register.

I make espresso shots
and steam milk
for their lattes.

I don't want to need
a backup plan
in case lacrosse
doesn't work out.

I just want to know
that this dream
will work out in the end.

I don't expect
to play lacrosse
for the rest of my life.

But if it can at least
help me pay for college,
that's something.

At least then I'll know
that what I'm good at
isn't useless—
like Mom thinks.

If It Doesn't Work Out

If the lacrosse
thing
doesn't work out,
then my parents
will choose my college
and my major
for me.

If they're paying
for school,
they'll make me
major in
something
that they think is
useful.

Finance or marketing.
Something practical.

If I can get a
lacrosse scholarship,
and if I can save up
enough money
to pay my own way,
then I can major in
whatever I want.

Even if I don't yet know
what I want.

If I save enough money
now,
they won't be able
to tell me
how to live my life
later.

Even if I don't know what
I want to study,
I know that I want
the freedom
to decide.

Sliding Grades

It's Monday,
and we're doing a team run
today.

We're going from our school
to the city park.
Around the lake at the center.

But Coach Cassie
pulls me aside
when I leave
the locker room.

The assistant coach
is going to lead
practice today.

Coach wants to talk to me
with my chemistry teacher,
Ms. Roberts.

Coach and I walk upstairs
to the chemistry lab.

I can feel my heart rate
going
up, up, up.

This morning
I handed in
a nearly blank
piece of paper
for my homework.

I'm sure
Ms. Roberts
is not amused.

The Meeting

I sit down at a desk
in the front row.
Coach sits in the seat
next to mine.

I'm working
really hard
to keep my breath
steady.

To not let
any tears
come into my eyes.

I'm Lacey Stewart.

And Lacey Stewart
does not cry.

Not in public,
anyway.

"Lacey,"
Ms. Roberts says
calmly.
"I'm worried
about you.
I know
you're smart.
So I'm not sure why
you handed this in."

She pulls out
the homework sheet.
I see my name at the top.

"I'm sorry, Ms. Roberts,"
I say.
"I was just really busy.
I won't let it happen again."

I force a smile,
and look Ms. Roberts
in the eye.

"Are you sure you're OK?"
she asks.

"Yeah, of course," I lie.
"I just got busy
this weekend.
I swear,
I won't let it
happen again."

Coach clears her throat.

"That's the other thing,
Lacey," she says.
"We need you
to keep your grades up
if you want to stay
on the team. If lacrosse
is taking too much
of your time
and energy,
we need to know."

I think my heart stops
for a moment.

I can't lose the team.

Lacrosse
is the only thing
that calms the worry
in my heart.

If I lose this,
then I don't think
I'll be able
to pull myself together.

I take a breath.

"I'll pull my grades back up,
I swear."

Ms. Roberts nods and smiles at me.
Coach smiles, but she is still
searching my face.
Not quite believing
my lie.

I go back to practice
in time to start running
defensive drills.

But my head is not
in the game.

I Try Harder

Monday night,
and I'm looking at my
chemistry
textbook.

All I can think about
is the fear that I'll lose
my spot on the team.

I write down answers
for half the sheet.
Then Mom calls me
downstairs for dinner.

"Lace,
you look stressed,"
she says.

I think for a moment
that she might care
about my anxiety issue.

Instead, she scoops me
some chili, and says,
"You'll get wrinkles
if you keep making
that face."

"It's just my homework,"
I say, trying to
keep my voice steady.

"Mom, it makes me panic.
I think something's
wrong with me."

I stare at my bowl
of chili.

I can't make eye contact
with my mom.

"Nothing's *wrong* with you,
Lace. It's all in your head."

I'm starting to hate
that line.

"If you want my advice,"
Dad says.
"You just gotta fake it
until you make it."

"You really need
to pull it together,
Lace,"
Mom says.
"If you ask me,
you're putting too much
energy into this lacrosse thing.
Think about your future."

I feel like
all I do lately
is think about my future.

Worry about my future.

Panic about my future.

They Don't Get It

I don't think
they realize
that this isn't
like any
other stress
I'm used
to feeling.

And it's
been happening
more
and more
lately.

Game Day

It's the day of
our first game.
A grudge match
against the team
that beat us out
for the championship
last season.

We all wear
our uniforms.

Yellow jerseys
with a blue-and-yellow
striped rugby shirt over it.

Navy-blue kilts
over black leggings.

Owen sees me
in the hallway.

He greets me
with a very
public kiss.

We are a power couple,
have been since freshman year.

I smile and for a moment,
everything feels OK.

But then Owen starts
a cheer
up and down
the hallway.

"What team?!"
he yells.

And the whole hallway
responds,

"Golden Tigers!"

He repeats the call
and response
a few more times
before the hallway
is really cheering.
I hide my face
in my locker.

I like the excitement.
And I love the sport.

But when they all
cheer like that,
it puts too much
pressure
on the outcome
of the game.

And then the thing I love most
becomes too
stressful to think about.

I take a long
breath
in   and   out.

I've gotten what I need
out of my locker.

So I put my game face
back on.

I make my way
up the hallway
as people wish me luck.

Hope for the Best

Jenna joins us
as we walk
into homeroom.

"You two going
to the party
at Emmi's
after the game?"
she asks.

Owen answers yes
for both of us.

I'm not sure
I want to go.
But the Lacey
that everyone knows
and loves
would go.

She would be the center
of attention.

So I guess I'll go
and pretend
to be that Lacey.

I guess I'll
hope for the best
and see
what happens.

Last Season

I was that happy girl
who loved
being in the middle
of everything.

I don't know
what changed.

Now I'm a tightly wound
ball of anxiety
all
the
time.

Tight

Sometimes
I feel like
the webbing
on my lacrosse stick.

My laces
pulled tight,
holding
everything
together.

Holding
it together,
until something
hits too hard.

And the string
snaps.
And the laces
unravel.
Until I can't
hold onto
anything.

But if I can restring
my lacrosse stick,
then I guess
I can pull myself
back together again, too.

What other choice do I have?

The Game

Before the game,
we all put our sticks in
a circle for a cheer.

"1...2...3,
Golden Tigers!"

And then the
entire team
lets out an
ear-shattering roar.

And from then on,
I am in my element:

running up
and down
the field,
scoring goals,
checking sticks.

No worries,
just instinct.

By halftime,
we're three
goals ahead.
And I've scored
two of those.

I take a tumble
while making a shot.

I can see turf burn
rising on my calf,
but I can't feel it yet.

All I feel
is the thrill
of the game
and the calm of
my passion.

I can feel the burn
as the game starts
moving again,
but I don't care.

Because all I
pay attention to
is the feeling
of doing the thing
I love most.

And then the thrill
of the first big win
of the season.

After the Game

Jenna's mom
gives me a ride home.

She never misses
Jenna's games.

Neither of my parents
have been to even one
of my games.

I get home,
shower, wash my hair,
and find a cute dress.

"Oh, what happened
to your leg?"
Mom asks when
she sees the turf burn.

"Battle wound
from the game,"
I say.
It hurts a little,
but it will heal.

"We won,
by the way."

"What a mess,"
Mom says
just loud enough
so I can hear it.

The Party

That calm from the game
is gone by the time
I leave my house
to go to Emmi's party.

As Owen's car
pulls up,
I have a
bad feeling.

I have a tight ball
in my stomach
almost
all the time now.

But I step
out the door
anyway.

I get in the car anyway.

If I let that feeling
in my stomach
stop me
from doing things,

I'll never
leave the house.

At the Party

I don't really
like beer.
I don't like
how it tastes
or how
it bubbles.

I also don't really like
being drunk.

I don't like knowing
that I will probably
do something
stupid
and embarrassing.

That it could
show up
in a video or photo.

I fill a red cup
with water
from the tap.

I find Jenna so we can
team up for beer pong.

We play
our first game
against two guys
from the boys'
lacrosse team.

"Is that what passes for
aim on the boys' team?"
I ask.

Jenna and I
have already
hit four cups.
The boys
haven't hit any.

My lacrosse girls
are cheering for me.
I have my team
behind me.

Now that I'm here
and focusing
on the pong table,

I've forgotten
my worry.

Jenna and I win three games
before we let another team win.

We'd rather
hang out
and chat
on the couch.

We're talking about
our dream jobs.

Jenna will be an artist.
Owen will be a diplomat.
And I'll be a professional
lacrosse player.

Jenna doesn't tell me
that lacrosse isn't a real job.

She just tells me I'll be on the first
women's Olympic lacrosse team someday.

She always believes
in me.

Owen finds us,
throws himself
onto the couch,
and slings his arm
around my shoulder.

"Lacey,
you are just
the *best*,"
he says.

He's had too much to drink.
And his voice
is way too loud
to be indoors
and so close to my ear.

I tense up.

"Owen,
I love you,
but could you
chill?"
I snap at him.

I shrug his arm
off of my shoulders.

He pulls away
from me,
and then looks at me
with puppy-dog eyes.

I feel the panic
rising.

My chest tightening.
Tears already stinging
my eyes.

"I'm sorry,"
I mumble,
standing up
suddenly.

"Um, I'm just
gonna–"

And then I bolt.

I need fresh air.

I need to be alone
so that no one sees me
break down.

I go out
into the backyard.

I go out into
the cold grass,
where it's dark
and empty.

I hold my hands
flat on the ground.
Let the cold calm
my nerves.

The tears
start falling.
And I work hard to not
make a sound.

I would die
if anyone at this party
saw me like this.

I'm Sick of This

I'm sick of pretending
that I'm fine.

I'm sick of worrying
that I'll lose everything.

I'm sick of feeling
like everything's
about to go wrong.

But what can I do
other than keep going?

Back Inside

I pull myself
together.
Wipe my eyes
on my sleeve.
Head back inside
before anyone
can come
looking for me.

It looks like
most people
have left.

I was out there
for longer
than I realized.

Owen's asleep
on the couch
next to Jenna.

Jenna's drawing
in her sketchbook
as usual.

Emmi told us all
we can stay over,
so no one drives drunk.

I text my mom
to tell her I'm
crashing at
Jenna's.
That I'll be home
tomorrow morning.

There's a big, cushy,
comfy chair
next to the couch.
I fall asleep
with my legs hanging
over one arm
and a fleece
blanket covering me.

Panic attacks always
take the life
out of me.

The Thing About Work

The next day,
I'm at work–
and it's not
going well.

The thing
about work
is that customers
think they can
talk to me
however
they want.

Some lady
ordered three drinks,
and she says
I made them
all wrong.

I know I made
what she asked for,
but that doesn't
matter to her.

I stand still
behind the counter
while she screams at me.
As if I'm not a person.

She wants to know:
"What kind
of idiot
can't get a simple
drink order
right?"

She hasn't given me
a chance
to give her a free drink.
She just
wants someone
to yell at.

I know her anger isn't
about me.
But I'm gritting
my teeth
against panic.
And breath
that comes
too fast.

My supervisor
comes out
of the back room.

She steps in
to talk to the customer
and I go back
to making drinks.

It's busy,
and there's a line.
I have no time
to collect myself.

My coworker
yells an order back
to me.

I start to make
the espresso shot
and steam the milk.

My hands
are still shaking
from the woman
yelling at me—
I spill espresso
on the counter.

I finish making
the drink.
Go to clean
the milk-steaming wand.

Burn my hand
as soon as
I turn the knob.

It's all in my head.
It's all in my head.
I'm in my head.

I've been at work
less than
two hours.

I'm not sure how
I will make it
through the rest
of the shift.

I run the burn
under tap water
and then go to
make the next order.

"Lacey,
go take a break,"
my supervisor says,
and hands me
a tube of burn cream.
"And don't
pay any attention
to what that
woman said.
She just wanted
someone to yell at."

In the back room,
I fill a glass
with ice water
and sip it slowly.

I smooth burn cream
over the small part
of my finger
that touched
the hot metal.

It's not burned badly,
but the cream does
soothe the little pain

now that I've stopped
to feel it.

Always Wrong

"How was work?"
Mom asks
when she
picks me up
later.

"Not good,"
I say.
I tell her
about the customer
and the clumsiness
and the stress.

"Lace,
you can't let
those things
get to you,"
she says.
"You just have to
ignore these things
and move on."

Mom puts her hand
on my shoulder.

"Fake it til you
make it, right?"

I take a sharp breath in.

I should know
better
by now
than to bring this
up to her.

Maybe she's right.

Maybe I just need to
suck it up
and get over it.

Fake it.

I turn to look out
the car window.

Wipe away
the tears
before they can fall.
Before she can
yell at me
for being

too weak
too emotional
too messy.

New Strategy

I'm going to try
to do as my mom says.

My new strategy:
the next time
I feel the panic—
the wild heartbeat
and the shaking—

I'll ignore it.

Maybe she's right.

Maybe I will just get over it
if I try hard enough.

I'll try to fake it.

But how do you fake
something you can't
control?

Testing It Out

First period
Monday morning,
I have a chemistry
test.

I studied all
Saturday night
and Sunday
afternoon.

I'm as ready
as I'll ever be.

Ms. Roberts hands
the tests out.
My hands
shake so much
I can hardly
write my name
at the top
of the page.

By the time I get to
question two,
I can't breathe right.

I answer it
as best as I can.

By question three,
tears sting my eyes.

I wipe them away,
and hope no one notices.

"Are you OK?"
Ms. Roberts asks,
standing
over my shoulder.

"I'm fine," I say,
my voice shaking.
"It's just
allergies."

"OK," she says.
"But really,
if you want
to talk about anything,
if you're having
a rough time,
you can come
talk to me."

She walks away
and I go to
the next question.

I suck it up—
finish the test
and hand it in
five minutes
before the period ends.

I answered all the questions
on the test,
and I think I got them right.

Maybe Mom was right.

I leave the classroom,
and go to the bathroom—
my safe space.

And then I break down.

I hide until I stop shaking
and the tears
stop coming.

If this is what
I have to do
to get through
this year,
then I guess
that's what I'll do.

I can do this.

I can make this work.

I have no other choice.

Coping

I stop crying
and redo my makeup.

But I still feel
a little shaky
for the rest
of the school day.

I can barely
eat at lunch time.

Owen wants me
to quiz him
for his English test later.
But I really don't want
to talk to anyone at all.

I throw away
the rest of my food.
Go up to the art lab
on the third floor.

It's always quiet,
and no one will bother me.

Mr. Tate, the art teacher,
always tells us
we can come up here
to unwind or get work done
as long as he doesn't
have a class.

There are a couple
of seniors
working on art projects.
They have
headphones on
and ignore me
when I walk in.

I sit on a stool at a table
as far away
from anyone else
as I can be.

I put my head on the table
and feel the cool surface
on my cheek.

I can feel my shoulders
starting to relax.

Then the bell rings
and I jump.

Time to do it all again.

The Real Relaxation

After classes
are over,
I rush down
to the locker room.

Change into
my workout clothes.

Head to the field
ahead of my teammates.

Practice
doesn't start
for another
half hour.

I start
running laps
around
the field.

It's funny that
when I'm running
and breathing hard,
it's the only time
my breath
feels free.

I feel the stress
start to drop
from my shoulders.

By the time
my teammates show up,
I'm my happy self–
the Lacey
they all know
and love.

Practice Makes Progress

I've never
thrown myself
into practice
the way I do
today.

Today it's not
about the game.

It's not about winning.

It's not about skill.

Today it's about pushing
my body until
the stress
of the day
is all gone.

"Hey, Lace, slow down,"
Coach shouts to me.
"You're gonna
hurt yourself.
Save it
for the game!"

I ignore her,
and then regret it
about two minutes
later
when I turn my ankle
and wipe out.

But I jump
right up.
I get back
into the drill.

My ankle aches
for a few minutes,
but the pain fades
quickly.

It's not broken
or sprained.

I'm fine.

If lacrosse is
the one thing
that calms me,
then I'm not
going to
waste
a minute of it
lying
on the ground.

Routine

The rest
of the week
is like that.

Panicked,
stressful classes.

Tests
and homework.

And then
relief on the field.

My body is more
beaten up
than it has been
any other
lacrosse season
I've played.

But the next game,
Thursday
afternoon,
I score
more goals
than I've ever scored
in one game.

Coach keeps
telling me
to calm down.
Slow down.
Don't push it
too hard.

She keeps
telling me
that I'll reach
a breaking point.

But I worry
I'll reach
a different
breaking point
if I don't hit the field
like it's all that matters.

Flunked

Ms. Roberts hands back
our graded chem tests
on the last day
before spring break.

59%

A big
red F written
at the top of
the page.

Ms. Roberts
wants to talk
to me after class.

"Lacey,
this test puts you
on academic
probation.
You can't play on
a varsity team
if you're on probation,"
Ms. Roberts says.

"But Ms. Roberts..."
I say.

"I'm sorry, Lacey.
It's out of my
control now."

Last Shot

I find Coach
on the field
before I even
change for practice.

"Coach, I can't
lose the team.
Coach,
you have to help me."

There are tears
in my eyes,
but I don't care
how I look.

It's all over
anyway
if they kick me
off the team.

"Oh, Lacey,
I'm so sorry.
It's school policy.
I can't make
an exception.
I'm really
sorry."

"You're making
a really big
mistake,"
I spit out.
"You'll never
make it to championships
without me."

I turn and run,
leaving her
and the field behind.

She yells out
to me,
but I don't
want to hear
a thing she
has to say.

I pass my teammates
on their way to practice
but I don't
want to talk
to any of them
right now.

Spring Break

That night, there's another
party at Emmi's.

I don't want
to face
the questions
about my grades
or why I wasn't
at practice
today.

But I do
want to see Jenna
and Owen
before they go
on vacation.

Jenna's leaving for
Florida tomorrow.

And Owen's going
to visit
his grandparents
in California.

I'm staying home
for break this year.

Owen swings by
to pick me up.
I already
feel my heart
starting to beat
too fast.

I'm breathing like
I've been running up
and down the field.

I tell myself
to just ignore it.

"Hey babe,"
Owen says
as I get
in his yellow
Jeep Wrangler.
"How are you?
I heard..."

"I'm good,"
I snap
before he can
ask the question.

Owen looks at me funny.

"You sure you're good?"
he asks.
"You sound off."

"Yeah, I'm good,"
I say.
"Ready for spring
break!"

I force a smile.

"OK, well then—
let's go and get
this party started,"
he says, as he peels
away from the curb.

Not So Bad

As soon as
we arrive,
I follow Owen
to the fridge.
He gets
himself a beer.
I grab one too,
a can of Labatt Blue.

I had one once,
and didn't like it.
But maybe
this will make
me feel less shaky.

"Wait,
you're drinking?"
Owen asks,
as he opens
his beer.
"You sure you're OK?"
he asks again.

I open my beer.

Take a sip.

Manage
to swallow it
even though
it tastes so gross.

I'll drink it if it
can calm me down.

"I'm great,"
I say, and smile.
"Don't you think
it's time for me
to start having some fun?"

"Sure,"
he says,
smiling too.
He takes
another sip.
"About time!"

I follow Owen
into the next room
where someone has
put up a dartboard.

He calls next game,
and I drink my beer
and get another one
while I watch
him play.

I'm starting to feel
a little
weird.

"Nice aim,
loser,"
I say sarcastically
when Owen
misscs a shot.

He looks at me,
surprised, and
a little hurt.

Did that sound mcan?
I'm not sure.

Words are coming out
of my mouth
without me thinking
if I want to say
them or not.

I make a crack
about how Owen
isn't a loser,
just not MVP
material.

He doesn't laugh
like I think he will.
But I'm not worried
about it.

My shoulders
are more relaxed
than they've been
in a long time.

I'm feeling
good enough
and happy enough
that I get another beer.
It doesn't taste as bad
as the first two.

My lacrosse girls come up to me
to say they're sorry
about the team.
I just shrug them off,
make jokes,
trip over my words.

But then Owen wins
the game of darts.
Now it's my turn
to play against
him.

Darts

Usually
playing darts
stresses me out
because I'm not
really good at it.

And I hate being bad
at anything.

But this time,
Owen hands me
the darts
and I'm feeling
as cocky as I do
when I play
lacrosse
or
beer pong.

"You ready
to lose?"
I ask Owen.

"Yeah, right,"
he says.

"We'll see
about that."

Spoiler alert–
I lose by a lot.

A few times
I don't even
hit the board.

I hit the wall
next to the board,
making
small holes
each time
I miss.

But for the first time
in a while,
I'm not
worried
about looking
dumb.

Because he won
again,
Owen stays
to play
the next game.

I'm bored
with darts.

I wander off
to find
another beer.

I need to find
Jenna.

I need someone
who understands
me.

I need my
bcst friend.

My Best Friend

I find Jenna
sitting on the stairs.
She's drawing
in her
sketchbook.

Somehow she always
looks cool,
even when she's
ignoring everyone.

I think it's because
she knows who she is.

I used to know
who I was.

Jenna has a beer
by her side,
but she's focused
on her book.

"Jenna," I say,
sitting down
next to her.

I throw my arm
around her shoulder.

"You know
you're my best
friend, right?"

"Lace,
are you drunk?"
she asks.
I take another
sip of my beer.
"That's not like you."

She puts her sketchbook
down, and turns her head
to look at me.

"I don't understand
why everyone
is making such
a big deal
about this,"
I say.
"You all have been
drinking for years.
What's the
big deal?"

I pull my arm away
from her
and stand up
too quickly.

I'm worse
than I realize.

As I steady myself,
I knock Jenna's beer
over—
onto her sketchbook.

"Lace,
what the heck!?"
Jenna says.
I see tears
forming in her eyes.

She picks up
the beer can
and sketchbook.

"This sketchbook
has all my best work in it.
Some of these were
going to go
in the coffee shop
show.
Now I have to
start all over."

Jenna holds
the book
by the edge.

I watch
as beer drips
off of a drawing
of her mom and dad
and their dog
sitting on the couch.

"Oh my gosh,
Jenna,
I am so sorry.
I really
didn't mean to.
I'm sorry."

I stand by helplessly.

"Just go find
some paper towels
to clean
this all up,"
she says.
Glares at me.

It's a look I've never
seen on her face before.

I do feel bad,
but also
I'm surprised that this
isn't making
my heart race.

I'm not panicking.

Which is weird.

I'm not sure
if it's a good thing
or not.

Shouldn't I be
more worried
about hurting
my best friend?

I stumble
into the kitchen
and grab the roll
of paper towels
off of the counter.

I go back
to the stairway.
Start cleaning up
the stairs
while Jenna tries
to dry out
her sketchbook.

See what can be saved.

I look over
and I see
a beer-stained
drawing–
one of me
and Owen
at the lunch table
last semester.

She's only colored
the hair and the eyes.

My blond hair,
with the purple streak
that I used to have.

In the drawing,
Owen's green eyes
are twinkling
the way they do
when he tells
a joke.

I'm rolling my eyes
at whatever he
had just said.

"Jenna," I say,
"I'm so sorry—"

"Yeah, well,
that's not going
to change the fact
that you ruined
my entire sketchbook.

Honestly, I don't know
what's wrong with you
lately."

Jenna grabs the soaking wet
sketchbook
and storms out of the room.

I don't follow her.

I mean, what
would I say?

I don't know
what's wrong with me
lately, either.

First Hangover

The next morning,
I wake up
at 8 a.m.
in my bed
to my alarm
going off.

I'm not sure
how I got
home.

And I don't
remember
setting
my alarm.

Owen texts me,
You OK?

I'm in too much
of a hurry to respond.

I don't remember
ever having
a headache
like this.

I sit up
and suddenly
I feel like
I'm going
to throw up.

I rush
to the bathroom
and kneel
in front of
the toilet.

I think I'm
about to vomit
but nothing
comes up.

After
a few minutes,
I drink
some water from
the tap.

My stomach
is starting
to settle.

I drink
a little more
water.

My head still
pounds,
but now it's easier
to ignore.

I don't really
want to go to work,
but I need that money
for college.

I get dressed,
brush my hair,
and pull it back.

I'm out the door
just in time
to not
be late for work.

Work Through It

I'm on the register
while my coworker
makes the drinks.

The hangover makes
my hands shake.
I'm glad I'm
not on drink duty.

I'm so tired.
I just want
to go back
to sleep.

I down
a shot of espresso
as soon as I can.

I pour
the house coffee
from the canister,
and almost spill it
handing it
to the customer.

I'm barely getting through
this day.

On Saturday
mornings,
there are always
a zillion
breakfast orders.

I run
the register.

I toast
the bagels.

I heat up
egg-and-cheese
sandwiches.

It's so busy
I don't have time

to think about
how much
my head hurts.

Or feel bad
about ruining
Jenna's book.

Or worry that
I've ruined
our friendship for good.

Or think about
losing the lacrosse team.

Pretending not to be
anxious
is making my voice
higher and perkier.

I think I might be
friendlier than ever.

Customers are
definitely
tipping better
than ever.

I drink another
shot of espresso.

One customer
complains to me
about his drink
not tasting right.

He turns to the person
next to him and says,
"The workers here get
younger and dumber every year."

I feel like I've
been slapped.

But I force a smile
and apologize to him.
Tell him we'll
remake the drink,
free of charge.

Later, when it slows down
for a few minutes,
I turn to my coworker Amy,
and we roll our eyes.

Talk about how rude
some customers
can be
for no good reason.

"He said a monkey could get
a simple order right."

Amy sighs.

"I'd like to see him try
making drinks
all day
without one mistake."

That's the thing
about customers.
You can know
they're wrong
but you can't tell them
to their face.

That's what coworkers
are for.

I don't cry
at all today.

My voice
doesn't shake.

I breathe
normally.

My hangover
is gone
by the time I go
home.

When I get home,
I'm super tired.
I fall asleep
as soon as I sit down
in front of the TV.

Sometimes it's exhausting
being me.

Dinner with Mom and Dad

I wake up
on the couch
a few hours later
when Mom tells me
dinner's ready.

She made grilled cheese
sandwiches
with tomato soup.

I eat my sandwich
in silence.

Between
the hangover
and ignoring
the panic,
I'm super tired
and not chatty.

Mom's talking about
her design job
with the hotel.

She's super excited
and bubbly.

It all seems to be
working out
really well.

Dad pays attention
and asks
her questions
and gets excited
for her.

I'm happy
that she's happy.
But I don't know
how to
be interested
in her job
the way Dad is.

"You OK, sport?"
Dad asks me
while we clear
the table.

I'm getting
really tired
of people
asking me that
but not wanting
the real answer.

"Um, I failed
a chemistry
test."

"Lace, I *told* you,"
Mom says,
"You need
to start focusing
on school
instead of
that stupid game."

I feel like I've been
slapped again.
"Well, I've been
cut from the team,
so I guess you got
your wish."

Mom looks stunned.
Dad searches
for the right words.
Always the peacekeeper.

"It's probably for
the best,"
Dad says,
trying to sound
comforting.
"Maybe your grades
will be better
if you have more time."

I bite my lip.

I don't have
an argument.

I tell my parents
I'm tired and
going to bed
early.

That wasn't a lie.

I am so tired.

But once I
lie down,
I can't
get to sleep.

Too Much Thinking

I'm thinking about
the chemistry homework
that's due the day
I get back
from break.

I'm thinking,
what's the point
if I'm gonna fail
anyway?

And I'm thinking about
the lacrosse game
after break,
that I won't be able
to play in.

And I'm thinking about
how many things
I have to do,
but how little
I want
to do
most of them.

And then
I'm thinking
about how
I screwed up
Jenna's artwork
and I'm worried she's
going to hate me forever.

And then
I'm crying
and shaking and
not breathing.

The beer helped
last night.
But now it's like
all the panic
I didn't feel then
and didn't feel
all day at work is

catching

up

with

me.

Morning Run

I must
fall asleep
crying.

It's my default setting
these days.

I wake up early
the next morning
feeling drained
and thirsty.

I roll out of bed.

Change into
workout clothes.

Go downstairs
to drink
some water.

I lace up
my running shoes
and head
out the door.

I will outrun this.

I put my running playlist on
and leave the house
with Chance the Rapper
in my ears.

It's the warmest day
so far this spring.

Fifty-something degrees
and it rained
last night.

My favorite running weather.

I run from my house
to the ring road
at the park
a few blocks away.

I run a few laps
around the ring road,
and then back home.

For the first time
in a while,
I feel energized
and calm.

Apologies

Before I shower off,
I text Jenna.

Hey,
I'm really sorry
about
ruining your book.
Is there anything
I can do
to make it up
to you?

I plug my phone in
to charge,
and then hop
in the shower.

After I dry my hair
and get dressed,
I check my phone.

No text from Jenna.

And then my thoughts
start to overtake me.

Does she hate me?
Is she sick of me?
Will I be all alone forever?

Or am I just overthinking?

She and her family are
in Florida for break.
She probably
is super busy
having fun.

We're best friends,
and she
would tell me
if she was *really* mad.

Right?

No Answer

I know I need
to get homework
done.

I get myself ready
to do it.

And then
I don't open my book.

I lie back on my bed,
with my textbook
on my lap,
and let my eyes close.

My phone vibrates.

I want it to be Jenna.

It's *not* Jenna.
It's my Dad.

At the grocery store.
Do you need anything?
he asks.

Nope,
I text back.

I don't need anything
but my best friend.

I turn back
to my homework
but now I can't seem
to focus on the questions.

All I can think about
is why Jenna hasn't
texted me back.

It's been hours.

I type a text message:
*How's your
spring break going?*

But then I delete it.
I don't want
to sound clingy.

I don't want
her to know
that I'm worried
because then
I'll sound
insecure.

I know that's
probably stupid.

If Owen
were here,
he would remind me
that Jenna and I
are best friends.

He would remind me
that she could never
hate me.

I know that she's
probably
out swimming
without her phone.

Or she turned the ringer off.

Or her battery died.

Or maybe
she hates me
and never wants
to talk to me
again.

I know that worrying
about it is dumb.

But I don't know
what else to do.

Text Back

I'm tired all day
the next day.

Even while sleeping,
I dreamed
about arguing
with her.

Jenna texts me
after lunch.

I know you're sorry.
Not much anyone
can do about the artwork.
I'm sitting on the beach,
trying to draw some pieces
for the show.

I really screwed up.
I don't know
how to save
the friendship.

Jenna and I
have been best friends
since middle school.

We've had
our arguments
over the years,
but our friendship
has survived all of those
so far.

This can't be the end
of the friendship.

Can it?

I put my phone on silent.
I don't want
to hear from anyone else
I've offended
recently.

I just want to zone out
in front of the TV.

Warrior or Wimp

I'm in the living room,
watching
American Ninja Warrior,
when Mom gets home.

I'm imagining myself
in the obstacle course,
crushing it.

I used to feel like a warrior.
I used to feel like I could
withstand any obstacle.

Mom snaps me out
of my thoughts.

"Have you done
any of your homework?
Are you ready
to take the SAT
again?"
she asks.
"Or have you just
been sitting around,
watching this garbage
all day?"

She grabs the remote
off of the coffee table,
and flips to HGTV.

I get up and go upstairs.

It's not worth
arguing with her.

What's the Point?

Jenna's mad,
and Owen is
probably mad too,
after the way I've been
talking to him.

I wish he were here now
to wrap me in a big hug.

I want to text him,
but I don't know
what to say.

I don't know how
to make any of this right.

Everything is ruined.
I ruined everything.

I should probably focus
on the homework
that's due after break,
but honestly
what's the point?

I'm a failure
either way.

My Path

"I ran into your chemistry
teacher at the mall today,"
Mom says the next afternoon.
"She says you're failing
her class.
That's not OK,
Lacey."

"Do you think I want
to fail, Mom?"
I ask.

I'm so tired of all of this.
I'm so tired of fighting
with her,
with Jenna,
with my own mind.

"Sometimes it seems like it,"
Mom says.
"Sometimes it seems like you
just want to take your own path
no matter where it ends up!"

"And what path do you
want me on?"
I ask, my voice breaking.

"You keep telling me
I'm doing everything wrong,
all the time.
What do you even
want from me?"

"I want the best for you,"
Mom says.
"I want the world for you.
I want you to be happy."

"Then let me play lacrosse,"
I say,
all my anger and stress
coming out in my voice.
"It's the only thing
holding me together.

Listen when I tell you
what I think and feel.

Let me be me, and trust me
when I tell you that I am struggling
under the weight of
your expectations."

I don't wait for her to respond.
I just walk away.

Done with the Real World

I run a bubble bath
that smells like grapefruit
and sink down
into the warm water,
letting it cover my ears
to drown out
the sounds of
the real world.

I'm done dealing
with the real world.

Keeping My Head Above Water

The water
is getting cold
and the bubbles
are all gone
when I hear
a muffled noise.

I lift my head
all the way
out of the water.

Someone's knocking
at the bathroom door.

"Lacc? You in there?"
Dad asks.
"Your lacrosse coach
just called me.
She said she's
been trying
to call and hasn't
been able
to get ahold of you.

She says
it's important."

Three Missed Calls

I had my phone
on silent all day.

I got a few texts
from Owen,
and a couple
from the lacrosse team's
group chat, which are
mostly pictures from
my teammates' vacations.

I ignore the group chat
and decide to answer Owen's
texts later.

Coach Cassie left
three messages
in my voicemail.

Message One:
"Hey Lace,
it's Coach.
I'm calling to check in,
make sure you're doing OK.
Call me when you get this."

Why wouldn't I be OK?

I've been putting on
the perfect front.

Faking it so well.

Message Two:
"Lace, it's Coach again.
A couple of your teammates
mentioned that
they're worried
about you.
I just want to make sure
you're OK.

Please
give me a call."

Oh.

Oh no.

Message Three:
"Lacey, I'm getting worried.
Please at least text me
and let me know you're OK."

So much for keeping
it all hidden.

I hit the call button,
my hand shaking
as I hold the phone
to my ear.

Coach

Coach picks up
on the second ring.

"Lace? Hi, I'm glad
you called,"
she says.

"Hey, Coach, what's up?"
I ask.

"Lacey, I don't want
to bother you,
but I've been worried
about you all season.

I've heard from a few
of your classmates
that you haven't been
acting like yourself
recently."

"Did Jenna say something?"
I ask.

"No, I haven't heard
from her,"
Coach says.

"But I've heard from
several other girls.
That you've looked
spaced out,
drank too much
at a party,
seem to be...
struggling.

And I have eyes,
Lacey. I know
something's been up
all season.
It's not about chem."

She's right,
but I've been trying
to hide it for so long,
I'm tempted to keep
lying.

I think for a moment
before deciding
to be honest.

I'm just so tired.

I'm tired of faking.

I'm tired of lying.

"OK, so things
haven't been great,"
I say.
"But what am I
supposed to do about it?"

"You can talk to me,
Lace,"
Coach says.
"Tell me what's up.
I can only help
if I know
what's going on."

I think about this
for a moment.

"I can't lose the lacrosse team,
Coach.
It's the only good thing
I've got going for me."

"Then we need
to do something about
that," she says.

And I'm just so relieved
someone wants to help.

Honesty

I meet Coach at
Rosie's Juice and Smoothie
the next day.

I play with my straw
and don't make eye contact
while I tell her
what's been going on
since I failed the SAT
last semester.

"Mom says I should ignore my anxicty.
Dad says fake it til I make it.
So I tried that," I say.
"And I thought it was working.
But now Jenna and Owen
are both ticked off at mc.
And my grades are still dropping.
And if they drop any more,
I'll lose my spot on the team.

Coach, lacrosse is
the only time I feel good
about anything.
I can't get cut
from the team.

I just feel like
such a failure."

There are tears
in my eyes
when I finally look
her in the face.

Coach pulls a small
pack of tissues out
of her coat pocket.

And she lets me cry.

And it feels so good
to finally *feel* it.

Coach's Response

"Lacey,
I can tell you a few things.

One— I will see what I can do
about getting you back
on the team. I can't make
any promises though.

Two—you're not alone
for having panic attacks.

I've had them myself.

I can help you figure out
what you need to do to help
with that. I can talk to
your parents for you if you'd like.

Three—I think you should tell
your friends. They'll understand
more than you think.

They care about you.
Your team *cares* about you."

It's Nice to Know

that there's someone
who wants to help
and won't just tell me
I'm being dramatic
or not trying hard enough.

And it's nice to know
that someone knows
just what I'm going through.

And it's nice to know
that I don't have to hide
from everyone.

Timing

On my walk home,
I get another text message
from Owen.

I was going to text him
as soon as I got home.

Hey babe,
I haven't heard from you
in days.
Are we good?

I stop in my tracks.

I know I should've texted
him sooner.

I know what it must
feel like to him.

I just didn't know
what to say.

Yeah, we're good.
I miss you, can't wait
until you're back
in town.
See you Monday?
I have some stuff
I have to tell you.

It takes him
an hour and a half
to get back to me.

OK,
he finally texts back.

OK.

An "I'm Sorry" Gift

I'm out shopping
with Mom on the
Friday
before school
starts again.

We're at an
arts and crafts
store.

She's looking
at fabrics
for curtains
for the hotel rooms.

I'm wandering
around the store.

I'm not artistic,
so there's
nothing here
that really
interests me.

I turn down an aisle,
and I see the perfect
gift for Jenna.
Her favorite sketchbook,
and a set of pencils.

When we
get home,
I find a Sharpie
and write a note
on the first page.

I know this won't replace
your damaged artwork.
But I saw this and thought
of you. You're my best
friend, and you're such
a great artist!
I don't know what
I would do without you.
Love you!
-Lacey

Reunited

Jenna and I meet at the park
on Sunday
to run lacrosse drills.

Before we start,
I give her the book.
She reads the note,
pauses like she's
considering something,
and then hugs me tight.

"Lace, you're my best
friend too," she says.
"And this is such
a great gift.

Some days
I feel like
the only thing
I'm good at
is drawing.

Some days
my sketchbook
is all that
keeps me sane."

I look at her,
surprised.

She's good
at so many things!

She's a great lacrosse player.
And her grades
are so much
better than mine.

"I feel that way about
lacrosse,"
I say.
"Like it's the only
thing that makes the
hard stuff worth it
some days."

"Well then, let's
play some lacrosse,"
she says,
with a smile.

While we toss
the ball around,
I tell her
everything.

And she doesn't
judge me.

She doesn't
make me feel
worse for not
having it all together
right now.

She just listens,
like good friends do.

Back to School

On Monday,
classes
start again.

I find Owen
in the cafeteria
at lunchtime.

I'm glad
to have him
back in town.

I missed him
while he was away.

I missed his
goofy grin.

I missed his terrible puns.

And I missed how he
is always so excited to see me.

Except this time he's not.

Today he pulls back
when I go to hug him.

"Hi Lacey,
how was break?"
he asks,
arms crossed.

"It wasn't the best,"
I admit. It's time
for me to tell him,
and to apologize.

"Can we talk
somewhere more
private?"
I ask.

Got My Back

We walk to the gym
and sit at the top
of the bleachers.
Our spot.
There's no one else
around.

"I know I haven't been
the nicest person
lately,"
I say.

"Are you breaking up
with me?"
Owen asks when I pause.

"What? No,
I'm not,"
I say.
"Why would
you think that?"

I put my hand on his.

"You've been acting
weird for weeks.
And then when I was out
of town, I didn't
hear from you.
And then when I did
hear from you,
you basically said
'we need to talk.'
So I assumed..."

"Oh my gosh,
I am so sorry,
Owen.
I'm not breaking up
with you."

And then I tell him
about how worried
I am about the SATs
and chemistry
and my future.

And finally, I tell him
about my panic attacks.
How sometimes I feel like
I'm losing control.

"I'm definitely not
breaking up with you,"
I say after
I tell my story.

"Owen, you're one of
the best parts of my life.
I love you."

"I love you too,"
he says.
"Lace,
I've got your back.
You don't have to hide
your bad days
from me."

I sink into his arms
and exhale,
feeling so lucky.

Solutions

Coach makes me
sit down with her
and Ms. Roberts again.

This time we talk about
my panic, and the real
reason my schoolwork
has been so bad
this semester.

Ms. Roberts is so much
more understanding
that I expected.

"Why don't we
meet every week
so that we can really
make sure you're confident
with the material?"
she says.
"And you can always
email me if you have
a question
when you're at home."

Now I don't have to worry
about looking stupid
in front of
the whole class.

With this arrangement,
the school
will let me finish
the lacrosse
season.

I've got a team
behind me now.

I know I can
beat this.

Not as Helpful

I sit on our gray couch,
which matches the soft blue paint
of the living room.
A bowl of fake flowers
sits on the coffee table.
Everything is perfect,
in its place.

And I tell Mom
my whole messy
story.

She listens, then sighs.
"I still don't see
why you care so much
about a silly sport."

"It's part of who I am,"
I say.
"And I know I'm not perfect.
But I'm done trying to be.
From now on,
I can only do my best
to be me.

I am done trying to be
your picture-perfect
daughter."

I turn to go upstairs.

"Now if you'll excuse me,
I have to go study,"
I say.

Learning How to Cope

Today's the day.

Like game day,
but bigger.

Because
I'm scheduled to
take the SAT.

I'm nervous,
but Coach has helped
me with some ways to

cope,
express,
breathe.

When I asked her
how she learned these skills,
she told me
that she went to college
for psychology.

She wanted
to understand
what was happening
in her own brain.
Now I think
that maybe that's
what I want
to do.

Then maybe someday
I can help someone
the way Coach
has helped me.

Future Plans

Now that I have
some idea
of what I want
to go to college for,
I can see a path.

I didn't care much
about grades
when they only mattered
to my parents.

Now I know
that I can have a future
with lacrosse,
and with friends,
and maybe with
a degree
in psychology.

If I can have a career
where I can help people
like me,
maybe the future
won't be so scary.

The Test

I get through
the SAT without
panicking
too much.

My hands are
a little shaky,
but my heart beats
normally,
and I breathe.

I fill in the
answer bubble
for every question,
and write the essay.

I don't know how well I did.
But I feel better
about it than
the first time
I took it.

Only time will tell.

And these days,
I'm working on living
in the moment.

Champions

The day of the
championship game,
I'm ready
to crush it.

My mom still won't come
to my games.

I've accepted that she
may never give her approval.

But I find my dad in the stands.

And I know that Coach
is here.

And Owen
is holding up a sign.

And Jenna is
on my side.

And even Ms. Roberts
comes to cheer me on.

I'm ready to
win again.

And I do.

Coffee Shop Art Show

Owen and I walk
into Bean City.

It's full of Jenna's family,
along with both
the boys' and girls'
lacrosse teams,
and a bunch of other
people from school.

Before we get through
the door,
Jenna jumps on us,
bringing us into
a warm group hug.

After she lets us go,
we head toward
the back wall
where her drawings
hang proudly.

The biggest one,
right in the middle,
is a picture of the three of us
walking through the park.
I'm in the middle,
with one arm wrapped
around Owen,
and one wrapped
around Jenna.

We're each carrying a smoothie
and laughing.

I look at the tag
that lists the title.
She's titled it
with one word:
Family.

I understand then
that family is more
than blood.

It's who you choose,
and who keeps
choosing you back.

Like Lace

My name is Lacey,
and sometimes
I am like lace.

Sometimes I'm fragile,
and sometimes I tear.

Sometimes I need
a little extra care.

I am both tough
and soft.

I am still lightning
on the field,
but sometimes,
I need to slow down.

I am still here to win,
whenever I can.

But win or lose,

I know
who I am.

WANT TO KEEP READING?

If you liked this book, check out another book
from West 44 Books:

What If?
By Anna Russell

ISBN: 9781538382578

OFFBEAT: PART ONE

My thoughts don't bother me

　　　　　here.

Drumsticks resting
between middle-finger
knuckle and my thumb.
Pointer finger

　　　　r e l a x e d

against the wood. I hit
the snare.

> *tap*
> *taptaptap*
> *tap*
> *taptap*

Marching band beats.

When I'm drumming, things feel

　　　　　right.

Like finally fitting a puzzle piece
into its spot.

I AM

Joshua Baker.

Sixteen years old.

Future rock star.

The biggest

rock and roll fan

ever to live.

Training

      for

            perfection.

OFFBEAT: PART TWO

I feel the
rhythm
in my palm.

I close my eyes,
the song
building to the

best part:

the solo—

but I hear

a knock

at my bedroom door.

I feel sweat
between my eyebrows.

I can't:

speak,

lift my hands,

press pause.

If I don't finish,

the perfect puzzle will

fall

apart.

THE MANAGER

Dad walks in,
waving his hands at me.

He's like a manager.
Tells me which shows
I'm allowed to play.

I'm only the star.

Doesn't he get it?

      I have to finish
          this song.

"Joshua!" he screams.
I shake my head. My body

    m

      o

        v

       e

      s

even though I don't tell it to.

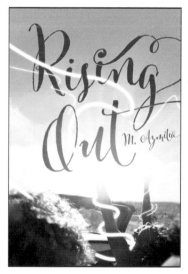

CHECK OUT MORE BOOKS AT:
www.west44books.com

An imprint of Enslow Publishing

WEST **44** BOOKS™

ABOUT THE AUTHOR

Lexi Bruce is the author of *More Than Anger*. She received a degree in English and creative writing from Canisius College in Buffalo, NY. She currently resides in the U.S. Virgin Islands. As a high school student, she struggled with anxiety, and wished she could be a star lacrosse player. Now she lives happily (and occasionally anxiously) as a writer/bookseller/greengrocer.